# WESTERN SCREEN LEGENDS
### COLORING BOOK

## Tim Foley

**Dover Publications, Inc.**
Mineola, New York

*This one is for my father, who never missed an opportunity
to fall asleep in his easy chair watching an old western on TV.*

Legendary actors and actresses who brought the days of the Old West to television and the silver screen during the 1950s and 1960s are featured in this impressive edition of 31 woodcut-style illustrations. John Wayne, Lee Van Cleef, Clint Eastwood, Gene Autry, Barbara Stanwyck, Chuck Connors, Vera Miles, James Arness, Roy Rogers, and Gary Cooper are some of the well-known names who play the famous gunslingers, lawmen, ranchers, and saloon keepers of the western genre that are included in this nostalgic collection. On the back of each of the realistic images is an informative caption that provides a brief biography of the movie star, including some of his or her most unforgettable roles. Enjoy a trip down memory lane for yourself or for someone you know, or pay homage to these western legends with your coloring skills. When you are finished, the pages are perforated for easy removal and display.

*Bibliographical Note*

*Western Screen Legends Coloring Book* is a new work, first published
by Dover Publications, Inc., in 2019.

*International Standard Book Number*

*ISBN-13: 978-0-486-82678-3*
*ISBN-10: 0-486-82678-3*

Manufactured in the United States by LSC Communications
82678301    2018
www.doverpublications.com

JAMES ARNESS

## JAMES ARNESS

James Arness's early career included many low-budget westerns and science fiction classics such as *Them* and *The Thing from Another World* (in which he played the creature), before landing his most famous role as Marshall Matt Dillon on the long-running western television series *Gunsmoke*, and afterwards the television series *How the West Was Won*.

GENE AUTRY

## GENE AUTRY

The famous "Singing Cowboy" got his start on radio, and then found success starring in serial westerns in the thirties and forties. Along came television, and he found equal success moving his formula to the small screen, producing the series *The Gene Autry Show*, *The Adventures of Champion*, and *Annie Oakley*. Autry was also a composer and songwriter with hits such as "Back in the Saddle Again," "That Silver Haired Daddy of Mine," and "Here Comes Santa Claus."

DODGE HOUSE

AMANDA BLAKE

## AMANDA BLAKE

Probably the woman with one of the longest-running roles on a western television series, Amanda Blake played "Miss Kitty" on *Gunsmoke* from 1955 to 1974 (and if that didn't keep her busy enough, she also appeared on the soap *The Edge of Night* several times from 1956 to 1971).

WALTER BRENNAN

## WALTER BRENNAN

An actor equally suited to playing comic sidekick roles as well as villains, Walter Brennan found a home in the Hollywood western early on in the silent film years, and he became one of its most beloved character actors. He won three Oscars for his acting, including one supporting award for his role as Judge Roy Bean in *The Westerner* alongside Gary Cooper. Like John Wayne, Brennan spent many years making low-budget westerns in the twenties and thirties before his big break with *Come and Get It* (his first Academy Award). Other memorable western roles include Old Man Clanton in John Ford's *My Darling Clementine*, *Along the Great Divide*, *Rio Bravo*, and *How the West Was Won*. Brennan also did his fair share of TV westerns, including *The Real McCoys*, *The Guns of Will Sonnett*, and appearances in *Dick Powell's Zane Grey Theatre* series.

CHUCK CONNORS

## CHUCK CONNORS

This tall character actor had a brief stint playing for the Chicago Cubs in 1951, where he was discovered and got a part in *Pat and Mike*, a golf-related romantic comedy starring Spencer Tracy and Katharine Hepburn. Many western roles followed, including William Wyler's *The Big Country* in 1958, but Connors was most famous for his role as Lucas McCain in the successful television series *The Rifleman*, which ran from 1958 to 1963.

GARY COOPER

## GARY COOPER

Gary Cooper's tight-lipped and plain-talking persona fit the American western to a tee, and besides a slew of hit films in a variety of genres, he seemed most at home in a cowboy hat. Most famous for the 1952 film *High Noon*, he also starred in *The Plainsman* (as Wild Bill Hickok), *The Westerner* (opposite Walter Brennan), *Garden of Evil*, *Vera Cruz*, and *Man of the West*.

**MARLENE DIETRICH**

## MARLENE DIETRICH

Born in Berlin, Germany, Marlene Dietrich made a name for herself in her native country in the silent films, then moved to Hollywood where she had initial success. In one of her more popular films, *Destry Rides Again*, Dietrich co-starred with James Stewart and played the role of "Frenchy," the saloon singer. Another western performance for her was in the film *Rancho Notorious*, but she was so successful as the "traditional dance hall chanteuse" that she was parodied famously by Madeline Kahn in Mel Brooks's *Blazing Saddles*.

ROBERT DUVALL

## ROBERT DUVALL

A veteran of television appearances in the early sixties, Robert Duvall's big movie break came as the mute "Boo Radley" in *To Kill a Mockingbird*. He appeared as the villain "Ned Pepper" in the John Wayne classic *True Grit*, and was a busy movie actor in the seventies, appearing in *The Godfather*, *Network*, *M*A*S*H*, and *Apocalypse Now*. Duvall's western roles included *The Great Northfield Minnesota Raid*, *Joe Kidd*, and *Lawman*. Duvall won an Oscar in 1983 for his role as a washed-up country singer in *Tender Mercies*. He will likely be best known to western fans as "Augustus McCrae" from the television miniseries *Lonesome Dove*.

CLINT EASTWOOD

## CLINT EASTWOOD

Getting his big break as Rowdy Yates in the television western *Rawhide*, Clint Eastwood took a job with Italian director Sergio Leone, who cast him as the enigmatic "Man With No Name" in a series of spaghetti westerns that made Eastwood an international star in the mid-1960s: *A Fistful of Dollars*, *For a Few Dollars More*, and *The Good, the Bad and the Ugly*. He came back to the States to star in several memorable and forgettable westerns and *Dirty Harry* films. Eastwood began to add "director" to his résumé and became one of the modern era's most recognizable western stars. Later films included *High Plains Drifter, The Outlaw Josey Wales* (which he also directed), *Pale Rider*, and *Unforgiven* (which was directed by Eastwood and won the Oscar for Best Picture in 1992).

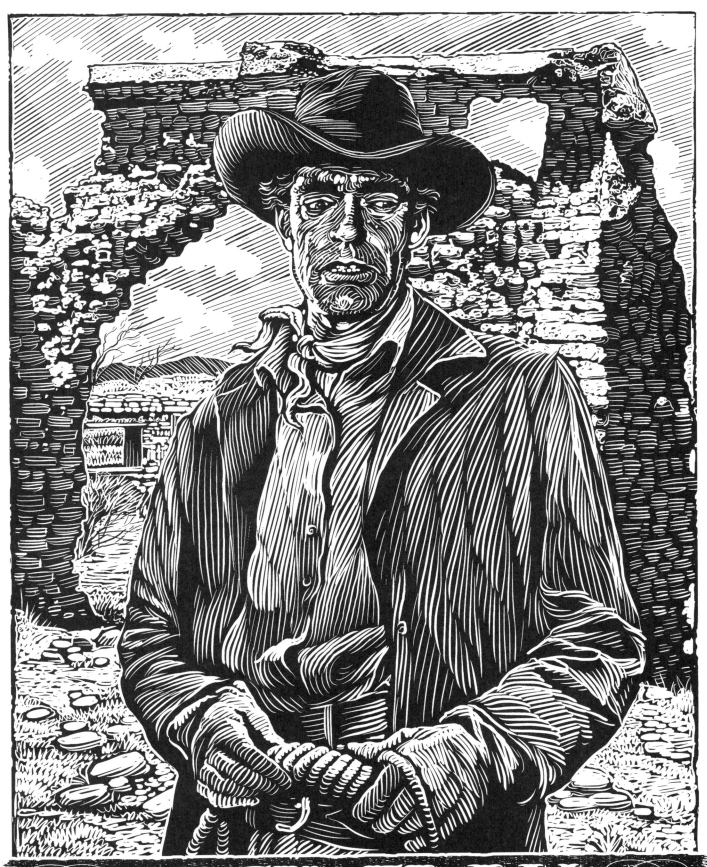

JACK ELAM

## JACK ELAM

You may not know his name, but his face is hard to forget. Jack Elam played a number of comic and villain roles in American western movies and television series starting in the mid-1940s. His films have included *Vera Cruz, The Man from Laramie, Wichita, Jubal, Gunfight at the O.K. Corral, Support Your Local Sheriff*, and a memorable role over the opening credits of Sergio Leone's *Once Upon a Time in the West*. Television credits are extensive with guest roles in such shows as *The Lone Ranger, The Texan, Dick Powell's Zane Grey Theatre, The Rifleman, Have Gun Will Travel, Rawhide, Lawman, The Dakotas*, and *Bonanza*.

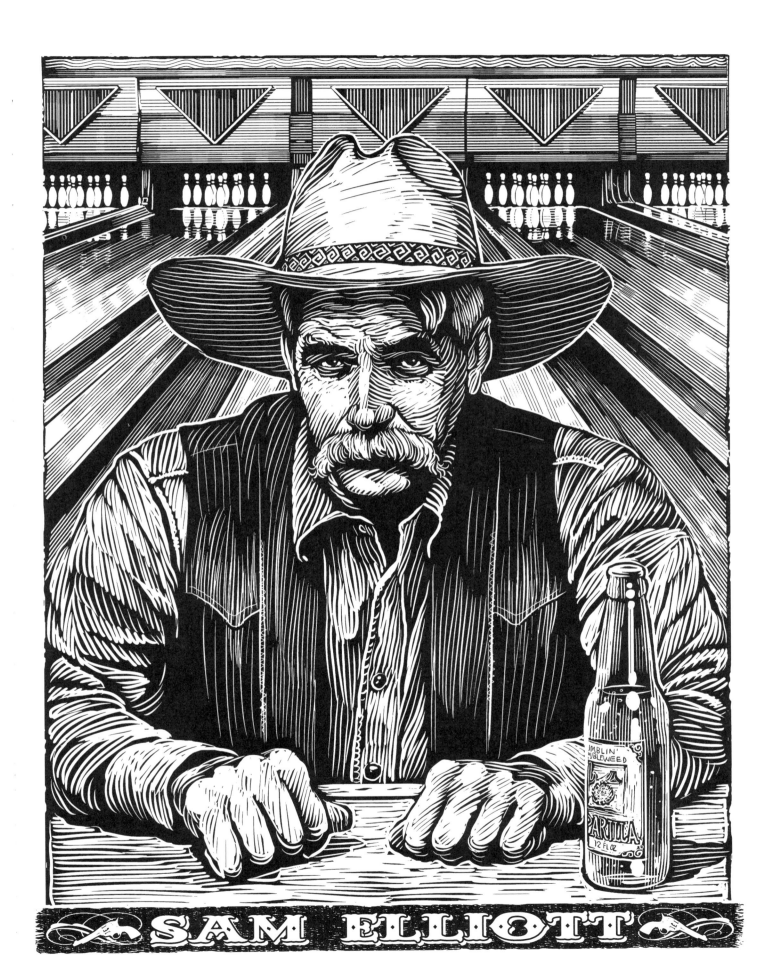

SAM ELLIOTT

## SAM ELLIOTT

Sam Elliott paid his dues in bit parts and television appearances for years (he had a small part in the opening sequence of *Butch Cassidy and the Sundance Kid*) before he caught the public's attention with his role as an aging lifeguard and beach bum in the film *Lifeguard* in 1976. He did a series of western miniseries and movies for television in the late seventies and eighties, including *The Sacketts*, *Wild Times*, *Murder in Texas*, *The Shadow Riders*, *The Quick and the Dead*, and *Rough Riders*. But he will likely be best known as the cowboy philosopher/narrator of the cult Coen Brothers classic, *The Big Lebowski*.

JAMES GARNER

## JAMES GARNER

Versatile and handsome leading man James Garner is probably best known for his role as Bret Maverick on the television series *Maverick* from 1957 to 1962, and later for his role as Jim Rockford in *The Rockford Files* from 1974 to 1980. He made a few memorable Hollywood westerns in the sixties and seventies, including *Support Your Local Gunfighter*, *Hour of the Gun* (as Wyatt Earp), and *A Man Called Sledge*.

LORNE GREENE

DAN BLOCKER · PERNELL ROBERTS · MICHAEL LANDON

## LORNE GREENE

Lorne Greene had a few low-budget westerns on his résumé, but he was mostly known as a television actor, with many successful series to his credit, including *Encounter, Sailor of Fortune, Battlestar Galactica,* and *Griff,* but he is best known as the patriarch of the Cartwright clan during the 14-year run of the western series *Bonanza.*

WILLIAM HOLDEN

## WILLIAM HOLDEN

William Holden was a versatile actor equally at home in war pictures, noir thrillers, adventure movies, romances, and comedies. He made several important westerns during his career, including the Sam Peckinpah classic *The Wild Bunch*, *Escape from Fort Bravo*, *The Horse Soldiers* (with John Wayne), and *Alvarez Kelly* (with Richard Widmark). He won an Oscar for his role as a prisoner of war in *Stalag 17*.

KATY JURADO

## KATY JURADO

Probably one of the most recognizable women in the traditional Hollywood western, Katy was discovered by John Wayne and director Budd Boetticher while working as a bullfighting critic. Her big breakout role as Gary Cooper's former mistress in *High Noon* led to many more roles in the western genre, including *Broken Lance, Arrowhead, One-Eyed Jacks,* and *Pat Garrett and Billy the Kid,* as well as many guest spots on western television series such as *The Rifleman, The Westerner, The Virginian,* and *Death Valley Days.*

ALAN LADD

## ALAN LADD

This American actor and producer is most famous to western fans for his portrayal of the title hero of *Shane* in the 1953 film. Ladd appeared in many other western roles including *Branded*, *Red Mountain*, *Drum Beat*, *The Big Land*, *Proud Rebel*, and *The Badlanders*.

CLEAVON LITTLE

## CLEAVON LITTLE

Cleavon Little began his career on stage in the late 1960s, earning both a Drama Desk Award and a Tony Award for his performance in *Purlie*. While appearing on the television series *Temperatures Rising* (1972 to 1974), he was cast in his signature role as Sheriff Bart, the town's new sheriff, for Mel Brooks's 1974 send-up western *Blazing Saddles*.

VERA MILES

## VERA MILES

Vera Miles appeared in two of John Ford's best films, *The Searchers* and *The Man Who Shot Liberty Valance*. She also appeared in many television westerns, including *Rawhide*, *Dick Powell's Zane Grey Theatre*, *Wagon Train*, *Gunsmoke*, *Bonanza*, and *The Virginian*.

MAUREEN O'HARA

### MAUREEN O'HARA

Born in County Dublin, Ireland, this fiery redhead starred in a fair number of western films, as well as finding success in other genres. She found work in such westerns as *Buffalo Bill* (with Joel McCrea), *Comanche Territory* (with Macdonald Carey), *The Redhead from Wyoming*, *War Arrow*, *The Deadly Companions*, and *The Rare Breed* (alongside James Stewart). She was paired with John Wayne in *Rio Grande*, *McLintock!*, *The Quiet Man*, and other movies.

JACK PALANCE

## JACK PALANCE

Mostly relegated to villain and supporting roles, Jack Palance found some success overseas as a leading actor in European westerns and gangster films. Most famous as the killer Jack Wilson in *Shane*, Palance got the last laugh when he won best supporting actor for his role as trail boss Curly in the comedy *City Slickers* in 1991.

ROY ROGERS & DALE EVANS

## ROY ROGERS & DALE EVANS

Roy Rogers performed in various musical groups, including the Sons of the Pioneers, and got his start as a bandit in the Gene Autry western *The Old Corral*. He went solo as one of many popular "singing cowboys" of the era, making almost 100 films. Known as "the King of the Cowboys," his television series, *The Roy Rogers Show*, ran from 1951 through 1957. Dale Evans was paired with Roy early on in his film career, and the two married in 1947. Frequently appearing on screen with the duo was their palomino horse, Trigger.

KATHARINE ROSS

## KATHARINE ROSS

Katharine Ross worked for many years in bit parts and guest shots on television, including roles on *Wagon Train*, *The Virginian*, *Gunsmoke*, *The Big Valley*, and *The Wild Wild West*. Then she was cast as Mrs. Robinson's daughter in *The Graduate*, and shortly thereafter as Etta Place in *Butch Cassidy and the Sundance Kid* (she reprised the role in a television movie called *Wanted: The Sundance Woman*). Other television movie westerns followed, including *The Shadow Riders*, *Rodeo Girl*, and *Conagher*. Katharine Ross married actor Sam Elliott in 1984.

RANDOLPH SCOTT

## RANDOLPH SCOTT

Durable western-leading-man Randolph Scott was discovered when he was hired to teach a Virginian dialect to Gary Cooper, and offered a contract by Paramount. Scott made many low-budget westerns throughout his career, but his best films were made with director Budd Boetticher, including *Ride Lonesome*, *Comanche Station*, *The Tall T*, and *Seven Men from Now*. In later years, he paired with aging Joel McCrea for one of Sam Peckinpah's early films, *Ride the High Country*.

BARBARA STANWYCK

## BARBARA STANWYCK

Known as a versatile actress who could adapt to any genre, Barbara Stanwyck had a 60-year career as an actress. She made over 80 films in Hollywood, including *Stella Dallas*, *The Lady Eve*, *Double Indemnity*, and *Sorry, Wrong Number*, before she turned to television. Stanwyck is probably best known to television viewers for her role as the matriarch of the Barkley family on *The Big Valley* series from 1965 through 1969. She also won three Emmy Awards, for *The Barbara Stanwyck Show*, *The Big Valley*, and *The Thorn Birds*.

JAMES STEWART

## JAMES STEWART

One of those beloved Hollywood actors who found success in a wide range of genres, James Stewart made a fair share of successful westerns during his long career. One of his earliest breakout roles (the same year he starred in *Mr. Smith Goes to Washington*) was as Tom Destry, Jr., in *Destry Rides Again* opposite Marlene Dietrich. Other memorable westerns include *Winchester '73, Broken Arrow, Bend in the River, The Naked Spur, The Man from Laramie, The Man Who Shot Liberty Valance* (with John Wayne), and *How the West Was Won.*

WOODY STRODE

## WOODY STRODE

Athlete-turned-actor Woody Strode is probably one of the most familiar African American faces in the Hollywood western, and was one of the Hollywood iconic faces that Sergio Leone used in his famous opening sequence to *Once Upon a Time in the West*. His films include *Sergeant Rutledge*, *The Man Who Shot Liberty Valance*, *The Professionals*, *Boot Hill*, *The Gatling Gun*, and *The Quick and the Dead*.

## WES STUDI

Native American actor Wes Studi had his big break in *Dances with Wolves* in 1990 and as Magua in *The Last of the Mohicans*, and he went on a few years later to play the title role in the historical western *Geronimo: An American Legend*. Other television roles include the documentary *500 Nations*, and the miniseries *Streets of Laredo* and *Comanche Moon*, as well as other films such as *Crazy Horse* and *Bury My Heart at Wounded Knee*.

LEE VAN CLEEF

## LEE VAN CLEEF

Often typecast as a western villain after his breakout role as one of the gunmen in *High Noon*, steely-gazed Lee Van Cleef found supporting work on movies and in television through the fifties. Movies included *The Man Who Shot Liberty Valance*, *Gunfight at the O.K. Corral*, and *The Tin Star*. He also guest-starred on TV western series, such as *The Range Rider*, *The Lone Ranger*, *The Gene Autry Show*, *The Rifleman*, *Death Valley Days*, and *The Adventures of Kit Carson*. Van Cleef found later success in the sixties after the Italian director Sergio Leone cast him as the lead in *For a Few Dollars More* (the sequel to the successful international hit *A Fistful of Dollars*), and then again a few years later in the film *The Good, the Bad and the Ugly*. Later, he enjoyed success in Europe in a string of "spaghetti westerns," gangster films, and martial arts movies.

JOHN WAYNE

## JOHN WAYNE

If anyone could be said to embody the quintessential western movie hero, it would have to be John Wayne. An actor since the days of the silent movie, he made over 70 low-budget films before getting his big break in 1939 with *Stagecoach* as the "Ringo Kid." He then went on to enjoy a long career of westerns, adventures, and war pictures, making some of his most memorable films with director John Ford, most notably in *The Searchers, The Man Who Shot Liberty Valance, Fort Apache, She Wore a Yellow Ribbon*, and *Rio Grande*. Wayne won an Oscar for his role as aging lawman Rooster Cogburn in the film *True Grit*.

RICHARD WIDMARK

## RICHARD WIDMARK

A versatile actor who was as comfortable playing villains and thugs as well as romantic leading men, Richard Widmark made his mark on the American western as well. *The Alamo, Yellow Sky, Garden of Evil, Broken Lance, The Last Wagon, How the West Was Won, The Death of a Gunfighter*, and *Warlock* are among his many westerns.

MARIE WINDSOR

## MARIE WINDSOR

While better known as a femme fatale in a number of film noir thrillers, most notably as Elisha Cook, Jr.,'s scheming wife in Stanley Kubrick's *The Killing*, Marie Windsor made her fair share of low-budget westerns and appearances on television shows. Windsor appeared in films such as *Hellfire*, *Dakota Lil*, *The Showdown*, *Frenchie*, *Outlaw Women*, and *Little Big Horn*, and she made numerous guest appearances on nearly every TV western series in the fifties and sixties.